Morris
the Artist

by Lore Segal

pictures by
Boris Kulikov

FRANCES FOSTER BOOKS · FARRAR, STRAUS AND GIROUX · NEW YORK

Text copyright © 2003 by Lore Segal
Illustrations copyright © 2003 by Boris Kulikov
All rights reserved
Distributed in Canada by Douglas & McIntyre Ltd.
Color separations by Hong Kong Scanner Arts
Printed and bound in the United States of America by Berryville Graphics
Designed by Barbara Grzeslo
First edition, 2003
1 3 5 7 9 10 8 6 4 2

Library of Congress Cataloging in Publication Data
Segal, Lore Groszmann.
   Morris the artist / Lore Segal ; pictures by Boris Kulikov.— 1st ed.
      p.   cm.
   Summary: Morris buys a set of paints as a birthday present for Benjamin, but he wants to keep
them for himself.
      ISBN 0-374-35063-9
   [1. Birthdays—Fiction.   2. Gifts—Fiction.   3. Painting—Fiction.]   I. Kulikov, Boris, 1966–
ill.

PZ7.S4527 Mo 2003
[E]—dc21
                                                                                        2002066295

For Maier, who kept saying, "That is not it at all. That is not what I meant at all."
And for Barbara Johnson, in whose garden we were sitting that evening,
after Kenneth's memorial service,
when Cynthia and I made up this story out of Maier's Jamesian germ.
And for Bernie, who napped   *L. S.*

For Frances *B. K.*

"Come," Morris's mother said to Morris.

Morris said, "I don't want to."

"Yes you do," said his mother. "You want to get a present for Benjamin's birthday."

"I want to paint," said Morris.

"Come along, Morris," his mother said. "NOW."

Morris's mother said, "How about a ball?"

"I've got a ball," said Morris.

"Morris, this is a present for Benjamin," said his mother. "Do you think Benjamin would like a dump truck?"

Morris said, "He does not want a dump truck."

"Would he like some blocks?"

"I know what Benjamin wants," said Morris.

Here come Rosie and Leah and Harry.
Here comes Morris.
They are going to Benjamin's birthday.

"Hey, a ball!" said Benjamin, the birthday boy, to Harry.

"Wow, a dump truck!" he said to Rosie.

"Look! Blocks!" he said to Leah.

"Tell everybody thank you," said Benjamin's mother.

Benjamin said, "Thank you," to everybody except Morris, because when the time came to give Benjamin his present, Morris said . . .

"No!"

"Morris!" said his mother. "Give Benjamin what you brought for him."

"I don't want to," said Morris.

"Yes you do," said his mother. "Give Benjamin his present. NOW!"

But Morris put the box behind his back.

"Never mind," said Benjamin's mother. "Let's all go and have birthday cake."

Benjamin's birthday cake was an ice-cream cake. It had a layer of chocolate, a layer of strawberry, and a layer of vanilla. Morris's slice had a chocolate heart on top of the icing.

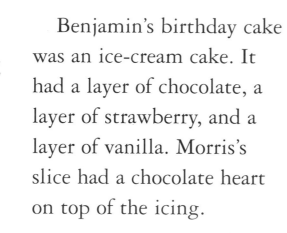

But Morris was holding the box on his lap, and his fork didn't reach the cake on his plate.

After the cake, everybody played with Benjamin's new toys. Benjamin threw the ball to Rosie, Rosie bounced it to Leah, and Leah threw it to Harry.

Morris wanted to throw it and bounce it, too, but . . .

he needed both hands to hold the box with Benjamin's present in it. He said, "Okay, Benjamin. You can have your present."

But Benjamin was building a tower. Morris wanted to put on the top block, but he was holding the box with Benjamin's present, and so he said, "Take your present, Benjamin!"

The tower had an opening at the bottom. Benjamin rolled the dump truck through the opening to Leah, who rolled it to Rosie,

who rolled it back to Benjamin. Morris wanted to roll it so much he said, "Benjamin! You take your present! NOW!"

But Benjamin was catching the ball Harry threw him, and rolled it over to Rosie through the opening in the tower, and Rosie bounced it to Leah, who put it on the dump truck.

And Morris held the box with Benjamin's present in it.

So Morris said, "*I'll* open it for you," and he untied the ribbon and took off the wrapping paper.

Harry said, "Hey! That's Benjamin's present!"

Rosie said, "You can't open Benjamin's present!"

"Benjamin! Look!" said Leah. "Morris is opening your present!"

"It's only paints," said Leah.

"Paints we get in school," said Rosie.

"I thought it was going to be something interesting," said Harry.

"Thank you, Morris," said Benjamin. "You want to catch?" and he threw Morris the ball.

But Morris said, "I want to paint." He opened the black jar and painted a big circle. "This is a picture of me," he said. He painted two circles side by side and said, "That's my eyes. This is my nose." He painted two red things like loops going down. He painted two red lines going across and said, "My mouth. My teeth." He opened the green jar and painted squiggles. "This is my green hair."

It was Morris!

"*I* want to paint," said Harry.

"So do I," said Leah.

"Me too!" and "Me too!" said
Rosie and Benjamin.

Harry painted a picture of a red dump truck with
red parts that went up and red parts that went down.

Leah painted a picture of a
beautiful ball with stripes and
stars and dots.

Rosie painted a picture of
a tower. She painted it red and
green and orange. She made a
part blue and a part dark blue.
She opened all the jars and in
each jar there was a new color:
There was umber and sepia and
olive and emerald. There was
rose madder and viridian and
turquoise, and more colors
when they got mixed together.
There was mauve and purple
and violet. There was aqua-
marine and cerulean and
brown.

Benjamin said, "I'm going to paint Leah." He painted Leah's chin purple, and Leah did an orange elephant on Harry's elbow, and Harry made a lot of pink stars on the palm of Rosie's hand, and Rosie painted a blue moon on Benjamin's forehead.

"This is so great!" said Benjamin.

"I know," Morris said. He took the fattest of the brushes and dipped it deep into the yellow jar, and on Benjamin the birthday boy's left knee he painted a yellow circle with circles inside it and lines coming out of it like rays. And on Benjamin's right knee he made more yellow circles with rays all around.

They were the two yellowest suns that you will ever see.